Break for the Basket

BREAK FOR

illustrations by
Foster Caddell

THE BASKET

by MATT CHRISTOPHER

Little, Brown and Company

BOSTON — TORONTO

J

LIBRARY OF CONGRESS CATALOG CARD NO. 60–9346

00232 07 PI

EIGHTH PRINTING

*Published simultaneously in Canada
by Little, Brown & Company (Canada) Limited*

PRINTED IN THE UNITED STATES OF AMERICA

Break for the Basket

1

EMMETT dribbled the ball in a fast break toward the basket. He lifted his right knee, sprang off his left foot, and pushed the ball up gently against the backboard. The ball banked through the hoop, struggled through the shriveled net, and dropped to the bare, hard ground.

Again Emmett got the ball. He dribbled toward the baseline, stopped, and pivoted back and forth on his left foot, pretending that he was faking a guard.

There was no guard — there were no players at all. Emmett was playing alone. He just pretended there were others, because it was a lot more fun that way.

Emmett rocked back and forth on his

pivot foot. Then he turned and leaped, lifting the ball high in an overhand shot for the basket. The ball arched gracefully. It struck the rim and bounced off. Emmett dashed for the rebound, caught it, and leaped for a layup. Swish! Basket.

He paused awhile, dribbling the ball high and easily so that he wouldn't have to bend over. He had been playing ever since he arrived home from school. He wasn't tired, though — just hungry, and a little lonesome. It really wasn't fun just to play by yourself all the time.

He left the ball on the frozen ground and went into the house. He was thirsty. He drank a glass of water, then looked at the clock above the kitchen sink. It was ticking away noisily, the only sound inside the big, quiet house.

Ten minutes of four. He sighed. Mom

and Dad wouldn't be home for another half-hour.

Emmett opened the refrigerator and looked at the food inside. He saw nothing he wanted. He closed the door. Then he placed a chair in front of the refrigerator, stood on the chair and opened the doors of the cabinet. He took out a box of crackers, pulled out a handful and returned the box. The crackers would hold him until Mom cooked supper.

He started to munch on the crackers when a sound outside drew his attention. He ran outdoors, slamming the door behind him, and then stopped as if he had struck a brick wall. A young blond-haired boy was playing with Emmett's basketball, dribbling it all over the court and shooting at the basket. Emmett's heart began to pound.

5

Emmett knew the boy. Then again, he wasn't sure whether he did or not. Mickey Dunbar and Robin Dunbar were twins who lived a couple of blocks away. They looked so much alike hardly anyone could tell which was which.

Emmett guessed that this was Robin — Robin Hood, as everybody called him. Robin Hood and Mickey were identical in looks — from their short, stocky builds to their blond brush cuts — but they were as different as night and day in other ways. Robin Hood was mischievous and happy-go-lucky. Mickey was quiet and serious.

Emmett didn't think that Mickey would pick up a basketball in a strange yard and start playing by himself. But Robin Hood would.

The boy sank a hook shot. As he turned under the backboard, he saw Emmett and a grin came across his round, pink-cheeked face.

"Hi!" he said. "This your ball?"

"Yes, it is," said Emmett.

Those hunger pangs were quickly gone. It wasn't the crackers that did it. He had eaten only one. The others were still in his hand. What did it was his shyness. He always became very shy every time someone whom he didn't know very well came near him, or talked to him.

"I'm Robin Hood Dunbar," the boy said. "You've seen me at school, haven't you? I've seen you."

"I thought it was you." Emmett grinned a little. "I wasn't sure at first."

Robin Hood laughed. "Boy, I didn't know you had a spot like this. This is neat."

Emmett finished chewing the cracker and swallowed it. He looked at the other

7

crackers in his hand, then pressed them into his coat pocket.

Robin kept playing by himself. He tried pivot shots, hook shots, and set shots. He seldom made them, but he was certainly enjoying himself.

Boy, he's got nerve, Emmett thought. And he hardly knows me! I wish he'd go away. He has no right to play here. That's *my* ball. This is *our* yard.

"Come on!" Robin Hood yelled to him. "Take some shots!"

Emmett shrugged. "That's okay," he said. "I've been playing."

It wasn't okay, but he didn't want to say so. And he didn't want to play with anybody around, especially Robin Hood Dunbar. Robin Hood played on a team and he was good. Emmett had seen him play in the intramurals in the school gym.

"Robin Hood! What have you got there?"

The shout came from across the street. Emmett turned and saw four boys coming in a run. He recognized them all, but he didn't know any of them personally. None of them were in his classroom.

They rushed into the yard as if they did it every day. Robin Hood passed the ball to a tall redheaded boy whose name was Rusty Kane. Rusty dribbled for the basket and laid it up. Another boy, Glenn Long, rushed in, caught the rebound, then dribbled around to the side and tried a set shot.

None of them paid the slightest attention to Emmett. They kept playing among themselves as if the place and the ball were theirs.

After playing ten minutes or so, Robin

Hood yelled, "Hey, Torrance! Come on and get in the fun!"

The other boys stopped briefly, and looked at Emmett.

"Never mind," said Emmett.

"Come on! Take a shot!"

Robin Hood passed the ball to him. Emmett yanked his hands quickly out of his pockets and caught the ball. He walked on the court, bounced the big rubber basketball a few times, then took a set shot. The ball hit the rim and bounced off. Emmett turned shyly away, putting his hands back into his pockets.

"Almost!" cried Robin Hood.

At the door Emmett turned and continued to watch. The boys were playing pretty hard — passing, dribbling, shooting baskets. He wished Mom and Dad would hurry home.

Presently there was a loud *swoosh!* and the ball crumbled lopsidedly to the ground.

"Hey!" yelled Rusty Kane. "It sprung a leak!"

Emmett froze. He stood staring at the ball as if he were glued to the ground.

2

ROBIN HOOD picked up the ball. It looked like a giant, overripe orange that had been stepped on.

"This is awful," said Robin Hood. "I suppose you want us to pay for busting it?"

Emmett swallowed. He took the ball. The boys clustered around him, looking at the ball with slack jaws.

Emmett turned the ball around and around in his hands, squeezing it in places in search for the hole. At last he found it — a jagged cut hardly the width of his little finger.

"Maybe we can patch it," suggested Rusty.

"Sure!" said Robin Hood. "That's an idea!"

He took the ball from Emmett. Emmett made an attempt to get it back, but he was too late.

"How are we going to blow it up after it's patched?" another boy asked.

"We'll use Joe Sutton's air hose," said Robin. "Come on!"

He started off at a run, the others following.

"That won't work!" Emmett cried out.

The boys stopped as if Emmett had yanked a string attached to them. "Why not?" said Robin.

"You need a valve," explained Emmett. "Wait a minute. I have one."

He ran into the house. He found the needle-like stem after a breathless search, then returned outdoors. He gave it to Robin Hood.

"Come along with us," said Robin.

"I don't want to," said Emmett. "My Mom and Dad are coming home pretty soon."

"Okay. We'll bring the ball back after it's fixed."

The boys ran off. Emmett thrust his hands gloomily into his pockets, spun on his heels and walked back to the house. What a fine thing. You never saw *him* run into some stranger's yard, pick up a basketball and play with it as if he owned it. And then, to add salt to the wound, as Mom would say, punch a hole in it, too. Of course, the boys hadn't done that on purpose. But they could have seen that the ball wasn't a very good one.

A noise from the house next door pecked annoyingly at Emmett's mind, but he was too angry to pay much attention to it. He was ready to open the door when he heard a crash. This time he looked. He forgot his anger. The noise came from the basement of Mrs. Maxwell's house.

Emmett ran across the frozen ground, leaped over the dwarf-sized hedgerow, then onto the Maxwell driveway. He almost fell against the side door.

He pounded against it with his fist.

"Mr. G.!" he shouted. "Mr. G.! Open up!"

He heard another crash. What was Mr. G. doing in there?

Emmett turned the knob and shoved his shoulder against the door. He almost went sprawling. With his hand still on the knob he stared at the sight in the room —

16

at the oil paintings strewn over the floor, torn and twisted. Then he stared at the man in the middle of the room, a small man with a narrow face and a long, sharp chin. His hair was fire-red, and thick as a lion's mane. His brows were black as tar, and his eyes a heaven-blue. Right now those eyes pierced the room with a look Emmett had never seen before.

"Mr. G.!" Emmett cried, afraid to advance any farther into the room. "What are you doing?"

Mr. G.'s chest heaved. "I'm smashing things, Emmett. Or shall I say, I've smashed them? I'm going to destroy every painting I've ever done, Emmett. Every last bit of them. They're no good. Not one of them is worth the cheap canvas they are painted on. And I've given it my life. My life, Emmett." He laughed. "Well, not exactly, because I am still here. Still alive. Not too old, not too young. But still alive. Close the door, Emmett. My paltry allowance is hardly enough to pay for the fuel to keep this place warm. I can't warm the outdoors, too."

Emmett closed the door. "I'm sorry, Mr. G." He looked at the paintings. There were four of them, all ruined. They had been hanging on the walls. Emmett knew he was too small and too young to know very much about paintings. But he thought that those which Mr. G. had painted were beautiful. One was of a horse and wagon going down an old road in the country. A boy and a girl sat on the high seat, looking at each other and smiling. Another was of a farm in the wintertime, with a car stuck in the deep snow and a horse trying to pull it out. The third one was of a little girl holding a kitten. The fourth was of a bell in a tower, and people below going to church. Emmett had never realized that anybody could paint pictures which could look so real. Now they were lying all over the floor, ripped apart by the man who had painted them.

Emmett stared at Mr. G. What had made him tear up such beautiful things? For a while Emmett didn't know what to say or do. He had never seen Mr. G. in such a bad temper.

"I'm no good, Emmett," Mr. G. said. "I'm going to quit painting." His voice was soft and kind again, just the way Emmett had always known it. The angry look in his eyes was gone.

"Oh, you can't, Mr. G.! You can't quit painting!"

Mr. G. smiled and put an arm around

Emmett. "I must, my friend. I must stop it right away and do something else. Give me a hand cleaning up this mess, will you, Emmett?"

"Sure, Mr. G."

Emmett began picking up.

"Did you *have* to tear up these beautiful paintings, Mr. G.?" said Emmett. "They weren't hurting anybody."

"I guess I was too disgusted to realize what I was doing, Emmett," said Mr. G. "It was a foolish thing to do. Very foolish. I see that now, and I'm a little sorry. Those paintings *were* rather beautiful, weren't they, Emmett?"

"They sure were, Mr. G."

Emmett sat on a chair near the table and looked at Mr. G. He had known the little red-haired man for almost a year, ever since Mr. G. had moved into Mrs.

Maxwell's basement apartment and had invited Emmett in to eat some of his home-made cookies. He had come from New York City and was attending an art school here in Westvale. Before that he had gone to a university and had studied art.

"It's my life," Mr. G. once had told Emmett. "I don't think there is anything I'd be happier doing than painting pictures. Look at Leonardo da Vinci. He was an inventor, but people will always remember him as the painter of *The Last Supper*. A good painting throbs with life, Emmett. It's a gift God has given me, and I feel obliged to make the most of it."

Emmett enjoyed visiting Mr. G. and listening to him talk about his work. Quite often Mr. G. would let Emmett watch him paint. But it was during his moments of rest that Mr. G. would sit and talk to Emmett as if he were talking to an old friend.

"I've been here almost a year, Emmett," Mr. G. had said only a few days ago. "I've sold two illustrations to magazines, and I've tried to peddle some pieces which I thought were really good art to stores and art collectors. They turned me down as if I were a beggar."

"How about painting people?" Emmett had asked.

"Portraits?" Mr. G.'s short laugh was a far from happy one. "People will give you five or ten dollars. They can't afford more. But there are those who can afford, and will pay well."

"Who are they, Mr. G.?"

"They are the ones who appreciate art, Emmett. They buy it to look at and have others look at for sheer enjoyment. Pick up a magazine, Emmett, and leaf through its pages. What attracts you instantly? The paintings, Emmett. Those beautiful illustrations that go along with the stories. They are the things that attract you first, that make you want to read the stories. Yes, Emmett, the field for an artist is wide, but it's a hard one. So hard that sometimes you want to give it up and start all over with something easier."

Emmett remembered those words now, and he said, "You won't really quit painting, will you, Mr. G.?"

Mr. G. looked unhappily at his hands. "I don't know, Emmett," he said dreamily. "I really don't know."

Presently Emmett heard new sounds outside. He looked out of the window. The boys were back. They had fixed his basketball, and were shooting it at the basket, playing more carefully now than they had before.

"I think I'll go, Mr. G.," Emmett said, forcing a smile.

Mr. G. returned the smile. "Thanks, Emmett. I'm grateful to you. I'm sorry you found me in one of my rare moods."

Emmett went out of the door and ran around the hedgerow to the court.

"Hi!" cried Robin, and passed the ball to Emmett. "It's patched up and works like new! Hey, how would you like to play on our team — the Penguins?" he continued. "We can use another sub."

Emmett stared. "Who? Me?"

The boys laughed. "Yes, you!" said Robin Hood. "We play in the Ice Cap League every Saturday morning at the Northside Community Hall."

A lump formed in Emmett's throat. At last he said, "I don't think so."

But he thought, *I'd like to! I'm just afraid!*

3

EMMETT didn't know what he was afraid of. He knew he was, that's all. It was just the way he had felt when Robin Hood had come into the yard without being invited. Emmett had gotten that strange, prickly feeling all over him. All he could think it might be was fear. He always felt that way, every time strangers came near him.

"You don't think so?" echoed Robin Hood. "Why not? Don't you like basketball?"

"Oh, sure, I like it," said Emmett.

"Then why don't you join us?"

Emmett shrugged. Now was his chance.

Why did he hesitate? Why didn't he say yes without worrying about what might happen next?

"Okay," he said. "I'll play."

"Good!" said Robin Hood. "Can you practice tomorrow after school? It'll be from four to five at the Northside."

The Northside Community Hall was a four-story brick building three blocks away. "I think so," said Emmett.

A car pulled up to the curb. Mom and Dad were home! And so were Charlene and Georgianne, his little sisters. They piled out of the back seat of the car, their curls bobbing on their shoulders. Both of them wore blue winter coats and hats and white mittens.

"Guess your folks are home," said Robin Hood. "So long! We'll see you tomorrow afternoon!" They started off at a run. "Oh, yes! Thanks for letting us play with your ball!"

Emmett waved to them, then went forward to meet his Mom and Dad. Charlene and Georgianne ran to him, and they both grabbed his legs. He couldn't move.

"Let go of me!" he shouted.

The girls laughed and let him go. Mom and Dad laughed, too. They put their arms around him and the three of them followed the girls up to the front door.

"Those boys looked familiar," Mrs. Torrance said as she opened the door. "But I've never seen them here before. Who are they?"

Emmett explained who they were, but all the time his stomach felt as if butterflies were inside of it.

He put away his basketball and hung up his coat and hat. Then he helped the girls remove their coats. They jabbered like little monkeys, telling all the things they had done during the day. Real crazy things, thought Emmett.

His mother hustled around the kitchen, from the cabinets to the refrigerator and the gas range. Once more hunger gnawed at Emmett's stomach, and he remembered the crackers.

He went to the hall closet, stuck his hand into his coat pocket, and hauled out the crackers he had put into it. They were all broken. He had forgotten all about them.

"What have you got there?" his mother exclaimed as she saw him come into the kitchen with the crumbled crackers.

He told her how hungry he had become, and about the boys coming over and playing with his basketball, about the hole in the ball and everything.

Then Emmett went into the living room to see his father, who was reading the evening paper.

"Robin Hood asked me to join their team, the Penguins," Emmett said.

His Dad glanced over the edge of the paper.

"What's that? A midget basketball league?"

"It's the Ice Cap League, Dad," said Emmett enthusiastically. "Our team's name is the Penguins."

"When does the team play?"

"Saturday mornings at the Northside Community Hall. Robin Hood said there's practice tomorrow after school —" Emmett rambled on like water gushing from a spout. And his father listened to every word, a warm smile on his lips.

Then Emmett remembered something that wasn't as pleasant. He told about Mr. G.

Mom had come in from the kitchen, and both she and Dad looked at Emmett in amazement. "What's gone wrong with that man?" Mom said. "Has he gone crazy?"

"Nobody is paying any attention to his paintings, so he figures he might as well give it up," said Dad.

"But destroy those beautiful creations?" said Mom. "Did you ever see them? They were magnificent!"

Dad shrugged. "I've seen them, and I agree with you. But an artist has a tough time selling his product these days. There are too many good ones. A man hasn't a chance unless he gets a break."

"How does he get a break?"

"That's a good question, and I can't answer it."

Emmett wasn't sure what they were talking about. Could Mr. G. sell those paintings to somebody if they were really good? Is that what Mom and Dad were saying? But, gee whiz, those paintings *were* really good, weren't they?

Emmett brushed the thought from his mind. He liked Mr. G. all right, but when it came to paintings he was lost.

"Okay. Set the table," said Mom. "Supper is ready."

Emmett could hardly wait.

Emmett carried his sneakers to the Community Hall with him the next day after school. The other Penguins were already there, dressed in their black satin uniforms. There were six of them. He would be the seventh man. Also present was a man sitting at the sidelines, watching with silent interest.

"Hi, Emmett!" shouted Rusty Kane.

Emmett waved. Then he thought he saw double, but it was the Dunbars — Robin Hood and Mickey.

One of them came forward. "Hi, Emmett! Want you to meet Mr. Long. He's our coach. Mr. Long, this is Emmett Torrance. He's joining our team."

Emmett did not need a second guess to know that this one was Robin Hood.

Mr. Long smiled and stretched out a hand. "Fine," he said. "Glad to have you with us, Emmett. Put on your sneakers and warm up with the boys."

Emmett put on his sneakers. He began to feel very strange again. On the court somebody passed the ball to him. It bounced out of his hands. He went after it, picked it up, and passed to Mickey. It was a poorly aimed throw. The ball hit the wall and bounced back onto the court.

One of the boys laughed. Emmett blushed. That cold, terrible feeling crept back into him, stronger than ever.

4

EMMETT watched the basketball pass from one player to another, until someone dribbled up to the basket and shot. He stood by like a store dummy. He felt foolish wearing his long pants and a shirt while the others wore their black satin uniforms.

Had Robin Hood really meant it when he had asked Emmett to come to practice? Had he asked Emmett just to be nice, really hoping that Emmett would not come? Was that it? Emmett wished he knew, and found himself wondering whether he could trust Robin Hood.

When practice was over Mr. Long got up and the team clustered around him.

"Well, you boys are shaping up fine," he said. "Maybe we'll take the Eskimos Saturday morning." He looked at Emmett. "Get a pair of black trunks and a jersey, young fella. Be here Saturday A.M., nine-thirty sharp."

Emmett went home, the cold night wind biting his cheeks. Tiny flakes of snow began whipping against his face. He had forgotten that he had to have trunks and a jersey to play on a team.

He was glad when he reached home and the comfortable warmth of the living room.

"Well, how did you do?" his Dad asked. Dad was on his hands and knees on the floor. Both Charlene and Georgianne were on his back, "riding" him around.

Emmett shrugged. "Okay." He was ashamed to say that the boys had hardly thrown the ball to him, and that when he did have it he was so clumsy that he had acted as if he had never handled a basketball.

"What about your suit?" said his Dad.

Emmett looked up in surprise.

"Well, you have to have a suit, don't you?" said his Dad.

Emmett nodded. "Yes. By Saturday morning. But — but where am I going to get a suit?" he stammered, hopelessly.

"I'll buy it for you," said his Dad. "What color do you need?"

"Black satin," said Emmett, suddenly feeling very happy. "The trunks and jersey are black satin. And I want Number 5 on my jersey. No one else has that number."

Friday evening, when Mr. Torrance came home from work, he had the suit with him. *Penguins* was printed in white letters across the front of the jersey, and the number 5 on the back. He had also bought a little brown bag in which Emmett could carry the uniform.

Emmett arose early Saturday morning. The thought of playing basketball had been on his mind part of the night. He had even dreamed about it. He dressed and went into the kitchen. His mother and father were having toast, coffee, and eggs for breakfast.

"Well, look at the early bird," said Mom. "You don't have to give me two guesses why you're up so early."

Emmett smiled. He had cereal and milk, then sat around waiting for the minutes to pass. It was only eight o'clock. Boy, how slowly time dragged.

"I'm going over to see Mr. G. a minute," he said finally. "Is that all right?"

His Mom shrugged. "He may still be asleep."

"Not him," said Mr. Torrance. "He's up at five-thirty every morning. He is a strange fellow if there ever was one."

Emmett could not understand why his Dad, or anybody else, talked that way about Mr. G. He couldn't see what there was peculiar about Mr. G. at all. Except that Mr. G. had very thick red hair which he seldom had cut, and he painted pictures. It wasn't easy to paint pictures. Mom and Dad couldn't do it.

"I'll just knock easy," Emmett said.

He put on his coat, hat, and mittens. He carried the little brown bag with his uniform inside of it to Mr. G.'s apartment and knocked lightly on Mr. G.'s door. He

40

knocked again, but there was no answer.

He was ready to believe that Mr. G. was asleep when the front door opened and Mrs. Maxwell stuck her head around the corner of the house.

"If you're looking for Mr. G., he isn't here," she said abruptly. "Matter of fact, he hasn't been home in three days. I don't know where he is."

She sounded angry and disgusted. She turned and went back into the house.

Mr. G. not home for three days? Where had he gone? Had he left the city without saying good-by? Was he that discouraged about his failure as a painter?

Emmett's heart ached. Mr. G. was a real friend. Emmett could not believe that Mr. G. would have left the city without at least saying good-by to him.

Emmett started walking toward the

Northside Community Hall. Presently he reached a corner. He looked to his right. Two blocks away a tall, orange-brick structure with pillars in front of it caught his eye. It was the Fenway Museum of Art, in which paintings of all descriptions hung on the walls. Many a time he would go there with Mr. G. Together they would look at the paintings. Sometimes they would spend hours there.

"It's like reading a book," Mr. G. had once explained. "I enjoy looking at paintings as much as I enjoy painting. It's a joy that fills the heart like soft rain in the summertime, or like reading the funnies on an early Sunday morning."

Emmett walked rapidly to the building. He walked up the long steps and then pulled open the tall, heavy door. The place was silent. He walked quietly across the carpeted floor. The eyes of the people in the paintings watched him as if they were alive.

He walked into another vast room filled with paintings of every size and of everything you could think of — paintings of a riverboat, a seashore, snow-capped mountains, people, and animals. Emmett began to feel that he wasn't alone any more.

A low, deep voice startled him. "Good morning, young fellow. Enjoying yourself?"

Emmett whirled. A gray-haired man in shirtsleeves was standing there with a broom and a dustpan.

"I'm looking for Mr. G.," said Emmett.

The man's brows arched. "Who?"

"Mr. G.," Emmett repeated. "A friend of mine. He's a painter. He's a little man, and he's got red hair. I'm looking for him."

The lines in the man's face deepened as he smiled. "Red hair? Why, that must be the fellow who was standing at the door when I opened up. Came in, browsed around awhile, then left."

"He was here?" Emmett's eyes widened. "When did he leave?"

"Just a few moments ago. Said he was going down to the lake to paint a picture."

Almost before saying thank you, Emmett turned and dashed out of the building. He raced down the steps and ran all the way to Crandall Lake, which wasn't too far. He stopped on its shore. It was a narrow lake and frozen all the way across. Emmett looked around the shore, at the bare trees and the empty picnic tables and benches. There was no sign of Mr. G.

A train whistle hooted like a sad wail in the distance. Emmett looked across the lake. A figure caught his eyes — a familiar figure — standing in the middle of the railroad tracks with a briefcase in his hand. He was looking the other way, at the buildings of the city stretching into the sky like mammoth rocks growing out of the earth, at the columns of smoke rising from a thousand chimneys, at the bright specks of lights that were windows touched by the morning sun.

So that was what Mr. G. had come to paint. Not the lake, but the city on the other side of the tracks.

"Mr. G.!" Emmett shouted. "Mr. G.!"

He started to run across the ice, the uniform bag still in his hand. He wanted to talk to Mr. G., ask him where he'd been these last three days. Maybe if Mr. G. didn't return to his apartment soon, Mrs. Maxwell might order him to leave. Could

he owe her rent? Was that why she was so angry?

Emmett got halfway across the lake when his foot sank down and *splush!* — he plunged through the ice!

His uniform bag skidded away. The next moment he was in the water up to his chest. Desperately he hung onto the jagged edges of the ice, while the cold water gnawed at his legs.

"Mr. G.!" he screamed. "Mr. G.!"

5

THE TRAIN whistled the same time that Emmett yelled. Mr. G. could not possibly have heard him.

"Mr. G.!" Emmett shouted again. "Mr. G.! Help!"

He got colder. Another piece of ice broke off the edge. Emmett pushed his arms out full length over the solid part and began to tread water to keep himself up.

Emmett screamed again. If Mr. G. didn't hear him now —

Mr. G. turned. Emmett lifted a hand and waved. "Mr. G.! Help! It's me! Emmett!"

The next instant Mr. G. jumped over the rail and down the high, cindered bank. He slid on his back. Then he was on his feet and running on the ice as fast as he could. And that wasn't fast, because he was slipping so much.

"Hang on, Emmett!" he said. "Hang on! I'll be right there!"

Emmett's arms were getting tired. But he would hold on until Mr. G. reached him. He just had to. He prayed that Mr. G. wouldn't plunge through the ice, too.

At last Mr. G. was there. "Jumping jack-rabbits!" he said. "What a fine time to go swimming!" He didn't get too close. He took off his coat, lay down on his stomach, and tossed a corner of his coat to Emmett.

"Grab hold, Emmett!" he said. "Grab hold and hang on tight!"

Emmett grabbed hold of the coat with one hand. Then he put both hands around it. Slowly Mr. G. crawled back on the ice,

pulling the coat with Emmett hanging on like a lobster. Seconds later Emmett was out of the water, dripping wet and cold.

"Th — thanks, Mr. G.!"

"Never mind that," said Mr. G. quickly. "We have to get you home where it's warm, or you'll catch pneumonia!"

"Nobody's home now. Could we go to your place?" Emmett was shivering.

"Sure, Emmett. Let me get your bag and we will be on our way."

Then Mr. G. put his coat over Emmett's shoulders and helped him to shore. A dozen people were on the frozen bank, watching anxiously.

"Quit staring like a pack of idiots!" shouted Mr. G. "If anyone wants to do a favor show us your car and take us home! This boy needs care immediately!"

"This way," a man said.

Emmett and Mr. G. entered the man's car, a four-door sedan. Mr. G. barked his address and the car took off.

"You should have had more sense than to run on that ice," said Mr. G. "Couldn't you see those places where it looked thin?"

Emmett shook his head. "N — no," he said.

When the car stopped, Mr. G. stepped out, then helped Emmett out. "Thank you very much," Mr. G. said to the driver. "I'll take care of him from here."

Mr. G. led Emmett into his apartment. He opened the heat valves in the radiators wide, then helped Emmett take off all of his clothes.

"A hot bath for you, and then into bed," said Mr. G.

The hot bath felt good. It took the cold out of Emmett, made him feel fresh and warm again. Mr. G. loaned Emmett his pajamas. They were just a little bit big for him.

"Pays for a grownup to be a shorty some-times," laughed Mr. G. "Now, crawl into bed. I'll make you a cup of hot chocolate, then go about drying your duds."

Mr. G. made the hot chocolate and gave it to Emmett. Then he rinsed out Emmett's clothes in the sink as much as he could.

"I'm going to ask Mrs. Maxwell to put these in her automatic dryer," he said at the door. "They'll be dry before you can say Peter Piper picked a peck of potatoes."

Emmett wondered if Mrs. Maxwell would let Mr. G. use her automatic dryer. He drank the hot chocolate while he waited. It warmed him thoroughly. A few moments later there was a drone upstairs and Emmett knew that the dryer was at work drying his clothes. And that Mrs. Maxwell wasn't so mad at Mr. G. after all.

Then a horrible thought struck him. The basketball game against the Eskimos!

He couldn't stay here in bed! He had to get to that game! The Penguins would never give him another chance if he failed to show up now!

6

MR. G. returned with Emmett's clothes. A broad smile formed half-moons around his mouth.

"Well, here you are. Clean and dry." His black brows arched as he leaned forward and whispered, "I told her you slipped on the ice, but I didn't tell her *where*."

Emmett grinned. He threw back the covers and started to get out of bed.

"Hold it," cautioned Mr. G. "Where do you think you're going?"

"The Penguins are playing basketball! I'm late already!" cried Emmett.

"Do you feel up to it? Are your chills all gone?"

"I feel fine! Honest, Mr. G.!"

"Okay. Get into your clothes. But if you start sneezing —"

"I won't, Mr. G. I know I won't."

Emmett yanked on his clothes, then looked up at Mr. G. "Mr. G., thank you for pulling me out of the lake. I guess I shouldn't have run out there."

Mr. G. chuckled dryly. "That's all right. I had just about decided not to make a painting of the city anyway. I was ready to come home when I heard you."

Emmett smiled. What a hectic morning this had been so far!

"See you, Mr. G.!" he said. He picked up his uniform bag and ran out of the door.

All sorts of crazy thoughts spilled through his mind as he ran all the way to the Northside Community Hall. What time was it? Why hadn't he thought about looking at the clock in Mr. G.'s apartment? Would the Penguins keep him on the team even though he was late? Maybe the game was already over! The horrifying thought made him run faster.

He soon reached the hall. Screams from the basketball court told him that the game was still on. He went inside the gym, recognized the Penguins on the court. He glanced at the electric scoreboard.

PENGUINS 29
ESKIMOS 27

Then he saw the green light just above the score. It was the last quarter!

Emmett saw Mr. Long, the coach, sitting near the table where the scorekeeper sat. Johnny Clark was sitting beside him. Emmett went to him. He trembled with nervousness, wondering if Mr. Long would even recognize him.

"Hey, it's Emmett Torrance!" Johnny shouted. "Where have you been?"

"I fell on the ice and got my clothes all wet," replied Emmett. He looked questioningly at Mr. Long.

"The fourth quarter has just started, Emmett," said the coach. "Hurry into your uniform."

"Thanks, Mr. Long!"

Emmett rushed into the dressing room, his heart thumping with excitement. He dressed in a jiffy. He felt awfully strange as he walked out onto the court. He had never worn a uniform before.

"Tell the scorekeeper you're going in for Mickey Dunbar," said Coach Long.

Emmett reported to the scorekeeper. When the whistle blew for a ball that had gone off the court, Emmett went in. He tapped Mickey on the shoulder. Mickey stared at him. "Hi, Emmett!" he said, and trotted off the floor.

Robin Hood passed the ball from out of bounds to Rusty Kane. Rusty dribbled across the middle line and passed to Glenn Long, a slender, dark-haired boy who was the coach's son. A guard crowded him as he tried to take a set shot. He passed to Emmett.

The pass surprised Emmett. He stood there, holding the ball nervously in his hands. He felt as if a thousand eyes were watching him.

"Shoot, Emmett!" a voice shouted across the din. "Shoot!"

He looked up. There was the rim, a bright orange ring with the white nylon net clinging underneath.

A guard sprang in front of him. Emmett dribbled to the right, stopped, then dribbled again.

Shreeek!

Double dribble!

Eskimos' out. They passed the ball in. A man dribbled across the center line and shot an overhand pass. Emmett raced hard down-court, wondering why he had double dribbled, for he knew better.

A try for a layup. Missed! Rusty Kane took the rebound and passed to Robin Hood. The Penguins moved the ball down the court. Glenn passed to Emmett. Emmett pivoted, gripped with that scared feeling again. He looked up at the basket, lifted his arms to shoot. A hand whacked his wrist. *Shreeek!* The whistle!

The referee lifted two fingers. Two shots!

61

7

EMMETT stood at the foul line, the ball held in both his hands. The referee was standing in front of him, waiting for the players to line up on both sides of the free-throw lane.

Emmett grew more nervous by the second. Beads of sweat shone on his brow. Everybody was watching him. He had never been the focus of attention before.

At last the referee moved out of the way, signaling for Emmett to shoot. Emmett looked at the basket, took a deep breath, and shot.

The ball struck high on the backboard, and bounced off. It barely hit the rim.

One more shot. The ball was now in

play. Emmett heard soft words of encouragement from Rusty and Robin Hood, but he was so nervous he wanted to get rid of the ball as quickly as he could. He aimed, and threw. The ball hardly arched. It struck the rim and glanced off. Both teams leaped for the rebound. An Eskimo player's long arms pulled the ball down. There was a wild scramble.

The whistle shrilled. Jump ball.

The tall Eskimo player outjumped Robin. Another Eskimo took the tap, dribbled away, then heaved a pass to a teammate running across the center line. Emmett saw that it was his man. He raced down-court, knowing that he should have kept his eyes open. He should have looked for his man immediately after he had missed his second foul shot.

The Eskimo player caught the pass,

dribbled up to his basket, and laid the ball up against the boards. It banked into the net as clean as could be.

The fans screamed. Emmett looked at the scoreboard. No wonder. The Eskimos had tied it up, 29 to 29! If he had made only one of those foul shots, the Penguins would still have remained ahead.

The Penguins took out the ball and moved it down-court. Rusty faked a shot to the basket, then passed to Robin. Robin pivoted and tried a two-handed overhand shot. The ball rolled around the rim and fell off. A quick roar rose and fell almost instantly. That was so close!

An Eskimo player took the rebound. Emmett started to reach for the ball, to try to pull it out of the other player's hand, but drew back. He was afraid he might foul.

He leaped away, then quickly followed his man toward the Eskimos' basket. A quick pass, a dribble, and then a pivot shot. In!

The whistle shrieked. Mickey came back in. "Okay, Emmett," he said. "Good game."

Emmett trotted off the court, not daring to look up. He hadn't done a thing right all those minutes he had been in the game.

"Cheer up," said Coach Long. "You'll make out all right."

The game ended with the Eskimos winning, 31 to 29.

There was a lot of chatter among the players in the shower room, but Emmett hardly said a word. He was anxious to get dressed and leave.

Mickey Dunbar walked home with him.

Mickey looked so much like Robin Hood, yet he acted so differently. Of the two, Emmett liked Mickey better.

"I guess I stunk," said Emmett.

"You weren't so bad," said Mickey. "You'll get used to it. It takes time. There's a non-league game at the Community Hall Tuesday night. Can you be there?"

"I'll try," said Emmett. "What time?"

"Six-thirty."

"Okay. Will you stop by? We'll walk over together."

"Okay."

Emmett arrived home in time to sit at the table and have dinner with his Mom, Dad, and his sisters. His Dad asked him how the basketball game had gone, and Emmett told him.

"How did you do?" asked his father.

"Rotten," replied Emmett.

Emmett felt better Tuesday night against the Arrows. The Arrows were in a different league. Rules did not permit teams in the same league to play exhibition games. There were only a handful of people there. Most of them were kids of Emmett's age.

When the game started, Emmett and Wayne Reese were on the bench. Johnny Clark, Glenn Long, Rusty Kane, Mickey and Robin Hood Dunbar were in the starting lineup. The Arrows took the tap from center and passed swiftly down-court. Traveling was called, and the Penguins took out the ball. Back upcourt it came. Mickey passed to Johnny, Johnny to Robin Hood. Robin dribbled in fast for a drive-in shot, laid the ball up against the boards, and sank it for the Penguins' first basket.

Seconds later Mickey sank a long set

shot. Then the Arrows scored on a pivot shot. And on a drive-in an Arrow forward got his wrist whacked by Robin Hood for a two-shot foul. The Arrow player made the first shot and missed the second. At the next whistle Coach Long took out Johnny and put in Emmett.

Emmett thought he was over that nervousness. But almost at once it was back, like a bad dream. He fumbled a pass, and Rusty yelled at him.

"Come on, Emmett! Hang on to 'em!"

At a mad scramble for the ball, Emmett stood back, afraid to join in. He found, as the game went along, that the boys were hardly throwing the ball to him. They were ignoring him, as if he were not there.

Once again the Penguins had the ball on their backcourt. But each man was well guarded. The Arrows were pressing.

Mickey had the ball. He dribbled, stopped, and looked for a man in the clear. There wasn't any — except Emmett. The Arrow man guarding him had probably realized, too, that Emmett wasn't much of a player. Nobody was throwing him the ball.

Then Mickey shot him a swift pass. The throw caught Emmett by surprise. But he glued his hands on the ball. For a quick second he looked for someone else to pass to. The Arrows' pressing play was like a heavy curtain. There wasn't a Penguin player in the clear.

Emmett faced the basket. Without aiming, he shot. The ball arched high. The next moment it sank through the hoop with a soft *swish!*

8

THE PENGUINS cheered. Robin Hood cheered loudest of all. He slapped Emmett on the back.

"A beauty!"

In the second quarter the Penguins piled up eight points, held the Arrows down to three. Emmett tried three times to duplicate the shot he had made in the first quarter, but failed each time. He played a couple of minutes in the third quarter, and didn't hit then, either.

He knew that shot had been a lucky one. He couldn't repeat it if he tried a hundred times.

Twice in the last quarter he missed a

layup. He knew he was going to miss even before he tried. Coach Long took him out and said that he was trying too hard.

Emmett didn't know what to think. How could he not try hard and still expect to play? What was he supposed to do to score points? Was this basket different from the one in his yard?

Somehow, playing basketball didn't seem like so much fun any more.

On Saturday the Penguins played the Seals, and edged them out by a one-point margin, 34 to 33. The following Saturday the Icebergs lagged in the game against the Penguins throughout the first half, then came back like wildfire and won, 39 to 24.

In both games Emmett played very little. There were two others besides himself who sat through most of the games more than they played, Johnny Clark and Wayne Reese. But warming the bench was better than nothing. And sometimes he did get in to play.

What hurt him most was knowing that he could do better. He was sure he could play as well as Rusty Kane, or even the Dunbars. Didn't he hit the basket at home most of the times that he tried layups? Didn't he hit those set shots more often, too?

Why couldn't he do it here?

In his heart, Emmett knew. He was scared, that was why. Scared and shy. He was scared he might miss, or foul, or not do something right. He was shy of the crowd. Yes, he knew, all right. He knew, too, that he would never get over that terrible, terrible feeling.

Snow covered the ground and the trees like a heavy white blanket as Christmas drew near. Mr. Torrance bought a Christmas tree, and Emmett helped decorate it with bulbs and tinsel. Gift packages in beautiful red, green, and white wrappings were piled underneath the tree. On Christmas morning they were unwrapped. Other gifts which Santa had brought had no wrappings. All that Christmas Day Charlene, Georgianne, and Emmett played with their brand-new toys and sang Christmas carols while their mother played the piano. And at supper they prayed to God and thanked Him for giving them a happy Christmas.

Mr. G. came over in the afternoon. He brought small gifts for each of the children, and then recited poems from memory. Most of them were funny, and the children laughed. Mrs. Torrance asked him to stay for supper. He did, but left immediately afterwards.

"He must be a lonely man," said Mrs. Torrance. "I wonder why he doesn't find himself a girl and get married."

Mr. Torrance chuckled. "Guess he's just a bachelor at heart."

"He likes to paint," said Emmett. "Maybe he thinks that if he gets married he'll have to work a lot harder and won't have time to paint."

His Mom laughed. "That could be exactly the reason," she said.

In early January the weather turned warm, and the snow melted. It filled the curbs with gushing water and made Crandall Lake swell and the ice break into pieces. Once again the yard was dry and clean. Emmett brought out his basketball and began playing by himself.

One Saturday afternoon, after the Penguins had taken a game from the Polar Bears, Mr. Torrance came out and watched Emmett dribble on the "court" and take shots at the basket. Presently Mr. G. came over, too, and Emmett got an idea.

"Will you two play with me?" he asked hopefully. "Will you pretend you're the defense?"

"Why, of course," said Mr. G. "Just try to get by us!"

Mr. G. and Mr. Torrance placed themselves between Emmett and the basket. Emmett began to dribble. He started to cut between his father and Mr. G. His father swiped at the ball. Emmett broke fast around him and went for the backcourt.

Mr. G. followed closely and flung up his arms to stop Emmett from shooting. Emmett leaped, lifted the ball high, and banked it against the boards. Swish! A basket!

"Beautiful play!" exclaimed Mr. G. "Let's try that again."

Emmett caught the ball as it floated down through the net. He dribbled it back to about where the foul line should be. He repeated the play. Again the layup was perfect.

"Good play!" cried Mr. G. "You hit like a pro."

"But I can't in a game," confessed Emmett. "I can't hit at all."

"There's something wrong, then," his father said. "You're doing all right here."

"Let me have that ball," said Mr. G. "See if you ever tried this shot."

Emmett tossed Mr. G. the ball. "All right. Guard me."

Emmett played Mr. G. close and smiled to himself. He felt sure that he could steal the ball away from Mr. G. without difficulty if he wanted to, for he was certain that Mr. G. had never played basketball.

But Mr. G. pulled a surprising thing. He started off dribbling slowly in front of Emmett. Then he shot past Emmett. Before Emmett could get close to him again, Mr. G. was driving in. He jumped, and lifted the ball underhand. The ball rose over the rim of the hoop, banked sharply, and riffled through the net.

"Hey! Nice shot!" cried Emmett. "Wow!"

Mr. G. chuckled. "It's been a long time," he said. "But that underhand drive-in shot used to be a favorite of mine. Might pay you to learn it."

"I will!" said Emmett.

He tried it and tried it until he did it almost as well as Mr. G. But to think that Mr. G. had played basketball! Emmett would never have guessed that!

Mr. Torrance tried some set shots and then some layups. He looked rusty, but Emmett watched him proudly. Anybody could tell that his Dad had played a lot of basketball in his younger years.

Mrs. Torrance called her husband in to get groceries. Mr. G. and Emmett played together until Mr. G. grew so tired he had to quit.

"I'm not in shape for this sort of thing," he said. "But you do all right, Emmett. You should be playing regularly."

"I don't," said Emmett. "I warm the bench most of the time."

"When do you play again?" asked Mr. G.

"Tuesday night, at Northside," said Emmett. "It's a non-league game."

"I'll try to be there," said Mr. G.

Emmett didn't really think that Mr. G. would go to the game. But at game time Mr. G. was sitting in the bleachers. As usual, Emmett started the game warming the bench. He finally took Wayne Reese's place and had several chances with the ball.

As usual, he became tense and worried. He hardly dared to shoot for fear he might miss the basket. He didn't try any layups, only set shots, hoping that luck would be with him again. But it wasn't.

He felt terrible. He looked terrible. He wished that Mr. G. hadn't come to see the game. Mr. G. would see now how poor a player he really was.

9

WHEN the first quarter ended, the Penguins trailed the Bucs 8 to 3. Mr. G. motioned to Emmett. Emmett toweled his face and neck, tossed the towel to Robin Hood, and went to see what Mr. G. wanted.

"How long have you played with these boys?" Mr. G. asked.

"Since before Christmas," Emmett said.

"How well do you know them? Do you play with them or talk with them any time between games?"

Emmett thought a while. "No. I hardly see them."

"Don't you see them in school?"

"Yes, but — we don't talk much."

Mr. G. nodded, as if he understood.

"If your coach lets you in there this second quarter," he said, "loosen up a bit. You're too tense. Do more running. And do more shooting. You had some chances that first quarter."

"I'll try," said Emmett.

The second quarter started with Emmett on the bench. This time Johnny Clark was playing forward. He dumped in two points, then was fouled as he tried to sink another. Two shots. He missed the first free throw, but sank the second. A minute before the quarter ended, Mr. Long had Emmett go in for Rusty Kane.

Emmett tried to keep Mr. G.'s suggestion firmly in the front of his mind. He ran more. Twice he was in the open, but neither time was the ball thrown to him.

At last he got a break. He intercepted a

pass from the Bucs, pivoted, shot the ball to Robin Hood, and streaked for the basket. Robin dribbled toward the right baseline, then leaped as if to try a long shot. Instead, he snapped an overhand pass to Emmett. Emmett caught the ball, made a fast break toward the basket, and leaped up. With his right hand he gently laid the ball up against the backboard. Swish! The ball banked into the net for two points.

"Thatago, Em!" shouted Robin Hood.

The Bucs took out the ball. They moved it down-court and across the center line. Emmett's man caught a pass and started to drive in. Anxiously, Emmett bolted in front of him. He hit the man's shoulder. *Shreeek!* A foul!

The referee held up one finger for the scorekeeper to note, and then five fingers to show who had committed the foul. Emmett raised his hand and shook his head glumly. He hadn't meant to guard his man that close. He had to be more careful.

The Bucs' player scored the shot. Then the horn blew, announcing the end of the first half.

The boys filed into the locker room. Coach Long followed them in. "Good game so far," he said. "Nice shot, Emmett. You surprised me. You should do that more often."

Emmett blushed. "Thanks," he said.

Mr. Long didn't say any more. Then the door opened again, and in came Mr. G. The whole team stared as the little man with the thick mop of red hair stood smiling in front of the door. He was smaller than Mr. Long, and only a couple of inches taller than Rusty Kane, the Penguins' center.

"Hi," he said. "Mind if I come in?"

None of the boys answered for a moment, as if stunned at seeing him in the room.

"Not at all." Mr. Long broke the awkward silence. "Come in. Aren't you Mr. Garfield, the painter?"

"Yes, I am," replied Mr. G. "At least, I'm Mr. Garfield." He smiled. "Most people know me as Mr. G. I suppose that's easier to remember."

Mr. Long put out his hand, and Mr. G. took it. "I'm glad to know you, Mr. G. I'm Ed Long. These are my boys. I guess you know your neighbor, Emmett Torrance." Then he went on introducing the rest of the team. "Frankly, I know very little about basketball," Mr. Long admitted. "The boys had to have a coach, so I volunteered."

Mr. G. smiled. "I don't like to interfere," he said, "but I think I could point out a few things to the boys that might improve their playing."

"I'll go along with that one hundred per cent," said Mr. Long.

"That'll be swell!" said Robin Hood. Emmett looked wide-eyed and happily at Mr. G.

"To begin with, you boys aren't guarding correctly," said Mr. G. "Most of the time you're in front of your man, but not between him and his basket. That's why they're breaking away from you so quickly and scoring points. Also, don't dribble just before you shoot. You're losing time and giving your opponent a chance to block your shot. Well, there are two things you can work on. I don't want to tell you too much now. Good luck!"

The boys thanked him. As they started out to begin the second half, Mr. G. reached out and clutched Emmett's arm. "And you," he said softly, "are tightening up like a drum again. Break loose from that thing that's gripping you. Don't be afraid to be yourself and play the way you really want to. As if you really mean it."

Emmett smiled. "I'll try, Mr. G."

Emmett started the second half. He tried to remember every word Mr. G. had said. He played hard, and scored a set shot and a foul shot before Mr. Long took him out. The other boys seemed like new men, too. Rusty uncorked a long shot that sank for two points, and Robin Hood dumped in two baskets in less than a minute.

The score kept piling up for the Penguins. The Bucs were caught flat-footed. They didn't score a point in the third quarter. In the fourth the Penguins kept rolling. When the game ended the Penguins were the victors, 31 to 24!

"Mr. G.," said Robin Hood, coming up the bleachers to stand in front of the little redheaded man, "will you be Mr. Long's assistant? You really helped us win this game."

"Please, Mr. G.!" cried Emmett. "Will you, please?"

Mr. G. stared. "But you have a coach."

"I could stand an assistant," Ed Long smiled. "How about it, Mr. G.?"

"I guess I'm outnumbered," said Mr. G. "Okay. I accept!"

10

"FOR my gratefulness to you boys for asking me to be Mr. Long's assistant," said Mr. G., "I invite you to my apartment after the game next Saturday morning. I'll treat you to a surprise dinner. Surprise, because I don't know what it'll be myself. How about it? Any takers?"

"Yes!" The reply came in a loud, single cry.

"You're invited, too, Ed," said Mr. G. to the coach. "Though you may prefer the more satisfying cooking of Mrs. Long."

Ed Long grinned. "If I'm not there," he said, "it won't be because of that."

The game against the Kodiak Bears Saturday morning started off with much life and spirit on the part of the Penguins. However, it was Johnny Clark who again started at forward. Emmett warmed the bench. He watched the game with uneasiness, for the Penguins and the Kodiaks were playing good ball. The score was tied, 6 to 6, when the first quarter ended.

Emmett took Johnny's place and Wayne Reese went in for Mickey when the horn sounded the start of the second quarter. Penguins' ball out. Wayne bounced it in from the out-of-bounds line to Robin Hood. Robin dribbled the ball toward the front of the court, then passed to Rusty. Rusty faked his guard and broke fast to the left baseline. He stopped, set himself, and shot a one-hander at the basket. It missed. Glenn Long and a Kodiak player went up for the rebound. Glenn snatched it from the other player's hands, came down on his feet, struggled free, and shot an underhand pass to Emmett.

The pass came unexpectedly. The ball struck Emmett's hands and bounded across the baseline.

"Come on, Emmett!" Glenn cried. "Wake up!"

The Kodiaks took out the ball and moved it upcourt. Hurriedly, Emmett ran down to guard his man. Missing Glenn's pass hurt him. He would try to make up for it.

He followed his man to the backcourt, saw him reach for a pass. Emmett began waving his arms hard in front of his man. It didn't do any good. The Kodiak player caught the ball and pivoted on his left foot to fake Emmett out of position. Emmett made weak motions with his arms, afraid that he might commit a foul. Then the player made a fast break past him, leaped, and pushed the ball up against the backboard. The ball riffled down through the net for two points.

Emmett stood back as Wayne took the ball from the referee's hand. The other Penguins ran down-court. Wayne bounced the ball in to Emmett. Emmett dribbled toward his front court, happy that he had the ball awhile, yet tight with fear at the same time. Would the team resent his dribbling a lot? Was he hogging the ball? He, who had been missing passes and letting his man pile up points.

Emmett dribbled across the center line. He looked for a free Penguin to pass to. The Kodiaks were guarding them all close. His own guard was pressing him. He saw Robin swing behind him, and heaved the ball to him.

Shreeek! Curiously, Emmett stared at the referee. The referee pointed at the center line, and Emmett realized what he had done. He had passed the ball back behind the line.

Kodiaks' ball out. They moved it down into their territory. Robin Hood stole it from Emmett's own man and dribbled it all the way down to the Penguins' basket. With the crowd shouting, Robin leaped, laid the ball up against the boards. Swish! Two points.

The horn blew. Emmett was taken out.

"You're stiff out there," said Mr. G. "Tight as a string. You're afraid to let yourself go, Emmett. You're afraid you're going to foul, or miss shots. You must get that out of your head. Forget about the people watching you. Don't worry about your teammates. They're not going to eat you.

They're not cannibals. Just be yourself, and play the way you played with me and your Dad."

Emmett listened, bewildered by Mr. G.'s words. Because Mr. G. was saying the exact things that had been bothering him on the court. He *was* afraid of fouling. He *was* afraid of missing shots. He *was* bothered by all the people watching. And he *was* worried what his teammates might say to him if he made mistakes. It was funny, but knowing that Mr. G. knew these things about him made Emmett feel much better.

Emmett got in for two minutes in the third quarter, and again about two minutes in the last. He scored one layup, a neat play that drew applause from the fans. The basket made him feel a little better. The Penguins won 38 to 37. Robin Hood got credit for 14 of those 38. But if Emmett had not scored that one basket, they would have lost.

The scorebook read:

Penguins (38)				Kodiaks (37)		
	G	F	P		G	F	P
M. Dunbar	2	3	7	Tuffer	5	1	11
R. Dunbar	6	2	14	Kirby	0	0	0
Kane	3	2	8	Peters	3	2	8
Long	3	1	7	Patton	2	1	5
Clark	0	0	0	Smith	3	3	9
Torrance	1	0	2	Nogami	0	0	0
Reese	0	0	0	Malone	1	2	4
Totals	15	8	38		14	9	37

Robin, Glenn, and Rusty kidded in the locker room about the dinner they were going to have at Mr. G.'s apartment.

"He's a funny-looking character," said Robin. "He reminds me of a redheaded woodpecker."

97

Glenn laughed. "Imagine him a painter, and knowing about basketball, too!"

Emmett didn't like their talking about Mr. G. that way. But he didn't dare to say anything to them.

Mr. G. was having trouble with his gas stove when the boys arrived at his apartment.

"Make yourselves at home," he said. "Dinner will be ready as soon as I get this stove perking correctly."

The boys walked leisurely around the large living room, admiring Mr. G.'s cactus plants and two paintings he had on the wall. Evidently Mr. G. had not destroyed every one of his paintings after all, thought Emmett with silent thanksgiving. Finally the boys became restless and impatient.

Robin Hood had brought the team's basketball with him. Glenn opened his arms invitingly, and Robin threw the ball to him. Glenn passed to Mickey. Emmett didn't think it was right that they should be throwing the basketball around in the room, but he soon joined in the game, too. Presently they were all laughing and throwing the ball harder at each other. Emmett caught it from Mickey, hurled it to Wayne.

Wayne was standing in front of a painting. He missed Emmett's fast peg. The ball struck the painting, knocking it to the floor. Emmett stared at it, his heart crushed. The painting was of a girl in her teens. It was torn in a couple of places where the ball had struck it.

11

MR. G. turned from the stove and came into the room. He looked at the painting silently. The boys stood motionless, an ache in their eyes as they watched the expression on Mr. G.'s face change from surprise to hurt.

He picked up the picture. His eyes blinked quickly a few times. Then he cracked a smile. Emmett could see that the smile didn't come from Mr. G.'s heart.

"It was my fault, Mr. G.," Emmett confessed. "I threw the ball."

"We were all throwing," said Mickey. "It wasn't just his fault, Mr. G."

"I'm not asking whose fault it was," replied Mr. G. "What's been done, has been done. Let's put away the ball and sit at the table. I've repaired the stove, and dinner should be ready in a little while."

When dinner was ready to serve, Mr. G. asked for help. Every one of the boys leaped at the call. Mr. G. said he needed only two, so he selected Emmett and Robin Hood. The dinner was composed of hamburg patties and buns, sweet pickles, Harvard beets, and milk. Afterwards there was ice cream. And then the boys helped Mr. G. do the dishes.

Then, for two hours, Mr. G. showed them games and played with them. They played and had so much fun that the time went by swiftly. But in those two hours Emmett had realized something more than fun with games. He had gotten to know his teammates better, to understand them, to like them, and — most of all — not to be afraid of them.

The boys put on their coats and hats, thanked Mr. G. for the dinner and for the wonderful time they had had, and departed. Emmett was the last to leave. He paused with his hand on the doorknob.

"I'm sorry again about that picture, Mr. G.," he said. "Can I pay for it, or something?"

Mr. G. smiled. "Don't let it bother you, Emmett," he said. "It wasn't good, anyway."

"I thought it was very nice," said Emmett. "Was it somebody you knew, Mr. G.?"

Mr. G. smiled and shrugged. "Hardly, Emmett. But don't worry about it. What I want to know is, did you have fun?"

"Yes, I did."

"How do you feel toward the boys, now? Are they still strangers to you?"

"No, sir, they aren't. Rusty is a lot of fun, and so is Robin Hood. I guess it means a lot once you know somebody, doesn't it, Mr. G.?"

"It certainly does," said Mr. G. "Good-by, Emmett. I'll see you again."

Emmett went home. He told his Mom and Dad about the dinner and all the fun he and the boys had had at Mr. G.'s basement apartment. Then he told about the painting he had struck with the basketball.

His mother and father were sorry about the painting, but felt there was really nothing that could be done about it.

"Cooking a dinner for the basketball team! I give Mr. G. a lot of credit for that," exclaimed Mr. Torrance.

Mrs. Torrance laughed and said, "I do too! I guess he got pretty well acquainted with you boys."

"That was exactly his reason for doing it, Mom," said Emmett. "Some of us didn't know each other well. And none of the team, except me, knew Mr. G."

He didn't want to say that he was the only boy on the team who didn't know the others well. Could this be the real reason why Mr. G. had put on the dinner? Emmett felt sure that it was. Mr. G. understood him pretty well, no doubt about that. Maybe when Mr. G. was a boy he had been shy and scared about many things, too. Emmett wondered if he would grow up and still be as shy as he was now. The thought frightened him. It wasn't fun to be shy.

Mickey and Robin Hood came over at

four o'clock. They invited Emmett to go to a movie with them. Emmett asked his mother, and she said he could.

After the movie the boys stopped at the Sunset Spa for a sundae. A girl with blue eyes and blond hair was behind the counter. As she started to fill the boys' orders, Emmett looked at her curiously.

The girl looked very familiar. Yet Emmett was sure he had not seen her before.

And then he remembered. She was the girl in Mr. G.'s painting.

12

EMMETT was so excited he spoke before he thought. "Do you know Mr. G.?"

The girl looked at him as she placed the sundaes in front of the boys. Her blue eyes twinkled.

"Mr. G.?" she echoed. "Who's Mr. G.?"

"His real name is Mr. Garfield," explained Emmett. "Mr. G. G. Garfield."

She thought a moment, then shook her head. "No, I don't. Am I supposed to?"

Emmett stared. He fumbled for an answer. "I don't know. He had a picture of you."

Then he blushed. If she didn't know Mr. G., he had spoken too much already!

"Not a picture," said Robin Hood. "A painting."

"A painting?" The blue eyes widened. "A painting of me?"

Emmett nodded. "At least, it looked like you."

"What do you mean, it *looked* like me?" asked the girl curiously. "Doesn't he have the painting any more? I'd be thrilled to see it."

Emmett was becoming more uncomfortable every minute. Why had he said anything about that painting?

"No. No, he doesn't," said Emmett quickly, hoping that would solve the problem. "It got torn, and Mr. G. had to throw it away."

"Oh, isn't that terrible!" said the girl disappointedly.

Her eyes flicked past Emmett's shoulder as the door of the ice cream bar opened on squeaking hinges. Emmett, Robin Hood, and Mickey turned their heads at the same time. Coming through the door was a small man with hair red as fire and thick as straw.

"Mr. G.!" exclaimed Emmett. No sooner had the words left his lips than he realized he had spoken too soon again. His face colored and he sunk so low on his stool he almost slid off.

He pitched his spoon into the ice cream, wanting to eat it all up quickly so that he could get out of there in a hurry. There were several mouthfuls left, and he couldn't leave until every bit of it was gone.

"Well, if it isn't my friends Mickey,

Robin Hood, and Emmett," greeted Mr. G. "Getting your vitamins?"

Emmett's grin was weak. "I guess so," he said. He gulped down another spoonful of ice cream.

"Are you Mr. G., the painter?" asked the girl, staring wide-eyed at the little man.

"Yes, I am," replied Mr. G., as he perched himself upon a stool. "A strawberry sundae, please."

The girl picked up a stemmed glass. "The boys told me you had a painting of a girl," she said. "A girl who looked like me."

Mr. G.'s face colored. He looked at the boys. "I guess that's quite true, now that I see you. The girl in the painting did look very much like you. A very strange coincidence — isn't it?"

"Why, yes, it is. You don't have the painting any more?"

"No. It was torn accidentally, so I destroyed it."

"Isn't that a shame," said the girl.

Emmett slid off the stool. "You fellas done?"

Mickey and Robin Hood got off their stools, too. "We'll see you again, Mr. G.," said Emmett.

Outside of the Sunset Spa Emmett ran his forefinger across his brow. "Boy! I bet that Mr. G. will be mad at me now!"

"I know that girl," said Robin Hood. "She's Mary Lee. Her brother goes to Cornell. He's on the basketball team."

Emmett's eyes popped wide. "You mean Tony Lee?"

"Yes. He plays football, basketball, and

baseball. Hey, that sister of his — she's pretty!"

On Tuesday night the Penguins played the Jet Wings in a non-league game. Neither Ed Long nor Mr. G. were present to coach the boys, so Robin Hood, as captain, took over the chore. He had Johnny Clark start, and put Emmett in Johnny's place two minutes before the first quarter ended.

Emmett remembered Mr. G.'s words of advice. *Tight as a string . . . Let yourself go . . . Don't worry about your teammates. They're not going to eat you.*

He went into the game without thinking about faults, without worrying about anything. He caught passes, dribbled, and pivoted with ease. And then he became bolder. He began driving and laying them up the way he did on his own court at home. He sank them, too, and Mickey, Robin Hood and the others yelled mightily at him.

Robin kept him in the full second quarter, and the full third. Emmett dumped in five baskets and scored one foul shot out of two tries. He sat out the fourth quarter, until there were two minutes to go. Robin had him go in again, this time in Glenn Long's place.

He stole the ball from a Jet Wings' man and dribbled all the way down the length of the court. He leaped. Swish! Another layup!

"Man! You're driving!" exclaimed Robin Hood as the Penguins proudly slapped Emmett on the shoulders after the win. "You're a different player! You were really hot tonight! I hope you'll be like this Saturday!"

"I don't know," said Emmett, hardly believing that it was himself in the game tonight. "But I'll try."

13

THE PENGUINS trailed the Eskimos by six points at the half that Saturday. Ed Long hadn't given Emmett much of a chance to play. At Robin Hood's suggestion Ed started Emmett in the second half. Almost immediately Emmett became the spark plug of the team, catching passes, rebounding, driving.

The margin narrowed. Soon the Penguins led, 21 to 20.

Eskimos' ball. They bounced it out from under the Penguins' basket, moved it cautiously across the center line, then passed. Swift as lightning, Robin Hood intercepted the throw, dribbled, then passed to Emmett. Emmett moved the ball down-court and passed to Mickey. Mickey tossed to Rusty. Rusty stopped quickly, setting himself for a shot. Two men blocked him. He bounce-passed to Emmett. Emmett dribbled up, leaped, and dumped in an overhand shot for two points.

Penguins — 23, Eskimos — 20.

Emmett ran back hard to find his man and cover him. His mind screamed at him, *Forget the people. Forget mistakes. Forget fouls. Robin Hood won't get sore. Nor will Mickey, nor Glenn, nor Rusty, nor the guys on the bench.*

He played on, thinking a lot about Mr. G. and what Mr. G. had said. He owed it all to Mr. G.

They beat the Eskimos, 28 to 24. Emmett had scored 7 points.

The next Saturday they trounced the Seals, 36 to 27. Robin racked up 11 points, Emmett 8.

"You've come a long way, Emmett," Mr. G. smiled. "I knew you could do it, once you dropped that bugaboo."

"You could do it, too. Just like me, Mr. G.," said Emmett.

Mr. G.'s mouth sagged a little. "Do what, Emmett?"

"Paint the best pictures in the world. What are you painting now, Mr. G.?"

Sadness paled Mr. G.'s blue eyes. "Nothing, Emmett. This time I've really given it up. I've given it up entirely."

Something happened to Emmett's playing the next Saturday. The Penguins played the Icebergs. Emmett started, but his passing was poor, and he was called twice on traveling. His breaks were not fast enough. His layups were hitting the rim and bouncing off.

Ed Long took him out and asked him if something was troubling him. Mr. G. asked him, too, but Emmett said that probably it was just an off day for him.

He was out a full quarter. In the second half he started again, but it was a repetition of the first quarter. In spite of Emmett, though, the Penguins kept the score pretty even with the Icebergs. It was not until the final seconds that the Bergs went ahead, 31 to 30, drawing a screaming yell from the fans.

Emmett saw that it was less than a minute to go. He bounced the ball out from behind the baseline to Rusty. Rusty passed it forward to Robin. Robin dribbled across the center line to the keyhole, pivoted, and passed to Emmett. Emmett knew that there were only seconds to go, now. He drove in. A hand whacked him across the wrist as he shot. The whistle shrilled.

A personal foul. Two shots.

The shot hadn't gone in, or the game would have been practically in the Penguins' hands.

The men lined up along the free-throw lane. The referee handed Emmett the ball.

Emmett took a deep breath. He dropped the ball once, caught it, aimed for the basket, and shot, pushing the ball with one hand. The ball struck the rim and bounced off.

"Come on, Em," whispered Robin. "Make this one. Tie it up!"

Emmett knew this was it. If he missed, the game would be over, and the Icebergs would be the winners.

He readied himself, aimed, and threw. The ball hit the backboard, then the rim, and bounced off! Two seconds later the game was over. The Icebergs won.

By the time the boys had showered and dressed, Ed Long and Mr. G. were gone. Emmett walked home with the team, sick with the feeling that he could have won the game during those last few seconds. He had certainly played a perfectly lousy game, he told himself.

They started past the Fenway Museum of Art. A large sign on the lawn next to the sidewalk that led up the steps of the building attracted Emmett's attention.

**FIFTH REGIONAL ART EXHIBITION
NOW OPEN
PRIZES AWARDED FOR
DISTINGUISHED WORKS IN
PAINTING, SCULPTURE, AND
CRAFTS
ENTER NOW
CONTEST CLOSES MARCH 10**

I wonder, thought Emmett, I wonder if Mr. G. would be interested in that?

14

A NON-LEAGUE game with the Fireballs on Tuesday evening was
played with only five men. Johnny Clark
was home with a bad cold. Wayne Reese
couldn't make it because he had two book
reports to write for English.

When the game was three minutes old,
Emmett wished he had homework to do,
too. He missed two layups, and let a Fire-
ball player steal the ball from him.

Robin Hood and Mickey were the only
ones playing good ball. Robin sank in two
and Mickey one, plus both tries of a personal foul, when the first quarter ended.

Penguins — 8, Fireballs — 3.

"Nice going, boys," said Ed Long. "Keep it up."

He didn't get off the bench. He just sat there, his elbows on his knees, his arms crossed. He spoke as if he felt he had to. Emmett liked Mr. Long, but Mr. Long definitely was no coach.

"Where's Mr. G.?" asked Robin. "Isn't he going to come any more?"

Emmett shrugged. "I don't know. I talked to him Sunday. He said he might come. He wasn't sure."

He had told Mr. G. about the big sign in front of the Fenway Museum of Art building. But Mr. G. hadn't seemed impressed.

"He's a funny character," said Mickey, smiling. "But I like him."

"And he knows basketball," said Robin Hood.

The second quarter was no better for Emmett. He was called on traveling, and twice fouled his man. The few fans who were there yelled at him. "Who's that doozy? Send 'im back to the hills!"

The Fireballs crept slowly forward. Their set shots began to hit. Their passes began to work. They moved ahead of the Penguins like a slow-moving bulldozer. Emmett wished something would happen to him so that he'd have an excuse to get out of the game. That terrible old feeling haunted him again. He was thinking about the fans yelling at him. Their voices were like gunshots blasting in his ears. He worried that Mickey, Robin Hood, and the others would get sore at him and ask him to quit the team. He didn't care how far behind the Penguins were. He only wished this terrible game was over.

Finally it was over. Emmett was exhausted. That night he had a horrible dream about basketball. He couldn't hit no matter how often he tried, and everybody was poking a finger at him and laughing as hard as he could. It was the worst dream Emmett had had in a long time.

Emmett was glad that the whole team was present that Saturday morning when they played the Kodiaks. He watched the first quarter from the bench. He started the second, substituting for Johnny Clark. He played the whole quarter and didn't take a shot. He only passed, and never kept the ball very long.

At one time he was open and Robin yelled for him to shoot. Emmett took a set shot and missed. He didn't run in for the rebound the way he should have. He just stood there like a wax figure.

"Come on, Em! Wake up!" cried Robin Hood. "What's happened to you?"

Emmett didn't say anything. He played only two minutes of the last quarter. The Kodiaks won, 30 to 25.

I knew I'd feel this way again! Emmett cried to himself — I knew it!

15

THE NEXT Saturday a warm, welcome face was among those behind the Penguins' bench. Bright red hair was brushed back like the brisk comb of a bantam rooster.

"Mr. G.!" exclaimed Emmett, as he ran out onto the court with the team. "It's Mr. G.!"

A grin sparkled Mr. G.'s face. Emmett and the boys ran over to him. "Boy! Am I glad to see you!"

"So are we!" said Robin Hood. "Where have you been?"

Mr. G. laughed. "I read about your recent losses in the paper," he said. "I felt you might need some immediate assistance."

"I guess we do!" replied Robin Hood. "This is our last league game. We have to win to get in the play-offs!"

"Jumping jackrabbits!" exclaimed Mr. G. "I guess we do!"

The game was against the Polar Bears, who were holding tight on to second place in the Ice Cap League. Emmett didn't go in until the game was three minutes old. He replaced Glenn. He took a pass from Mickey, dribbled down-court, pivoted, shot a quick overhand pass to Rusty. Rusty made a fast break for the basket, leaped, and laid one in. Two points!

The Polar Bears took out the ball and moved it upcourt. They passed back and forth, looking for an opening to drive.

Then a man took a set shot, but missed. Rusty and Robin went up for the rebound with two of the Bears' men. Rusty came down with it, an opponent's hand clamped on the ball. The whistle shrilled.

Jump ball.

A Bears' man took the tap. He dribbled away. Emmett ran up beside him and stole the ball from him! Emmett passed to Mickey and raced down the court. Mickey threw a long one back to him. Emmett leaped, pushing the ball against the boards. Two points!

"Yay!" screamed Robin Hood. "We're rolling now!"

And roll they did. Emmett stayed in for the rest of the game. They came out on top, 36 to 27.

"I guess you'll have to come to all of our games, Mr. G.," said Ed Long.

"You gave us luck," added Rusty. "You helped put us in the play-offs."

Mr. G. smiled. He stood beside Emmett and put an arm over Emmett's shoulders. "Not luck," he said. "Maybe inspiration, but not luck. I'm here to help this boy, too. You saw this morning what he can do. I want to make sure he can do it other times, too, when I'm not here. You fellows can. You've been used to it. Not Emmett. Emmett's been born with a sad case of shyness. Maybe you don't know what it is. But I do. It isn't fun being shy. However, he's getting over it. Aren't you, Emmett?"

"I — I guess so," said Emmett.

Mr. G. and Emmett walked home together. "Got some news for you, Emmett, my friend," said Mr. G. "I'm going home."

"Home?" Emmett stared. "Do you mean back home to New York? Why, Mr. G.?"

"My folks gave me money to come here and learn to be a painter. Well, I've failed. I can't take any more of their money, Emmett. I'm going back home, and find a job doing something."

Emmett's eyes ached. "I wish you wouldn't go, Mr. G. You really don't have to, do you?"

"No, I don't. I've met some nice friends. Especially young ones, like you. But I should."

Emmett began thinking hard. After a long while he said, "Mr. G., will you do something for me, first? Will you paint a picture of me?"

"Of you?" Mr. G.'s eyes widened in amazement, and then his lips parted in a friendly grin. "Well, bless my soul, Emmett! Bless my very soul!"

"Will you?" Emmett asked again.

"Well —" Mr. G. paused. He thought deeply. Then he said, "All right. You're my best friend. For you I'll paint a picture. I'll paint the very best picture I can."

He started that afternoon, painting Emmett's picture while Emmett sat on a chair in front of him. He continued painting the next day and the next. Each day, after school, Emmett sat in front of Mr. G. for half an hour. By the end of the week the painting was completed.

"Now you may look at it," smiled Mr. G., for he hadn't let Emmett look at the painting while he'd been working.

Emmett's heart sang with pride. He looked at the picture. What a surprise! Mr. G. had painted him shooting a basket! He was in his Penguins' uniform, leaping up,

the ball just leaving his hands. In the background were blurred faces of other players and fans.

"I was just sitting here," murmured Emmett breathlessly. "How could you paint me doing this?"

Mr. G. smiled. "Do you like it? Are you satisfied?"

"I love it, Mr. G.! Thank you!"

Emmett held the precious painting against him as he carried it home. He showed it to his Mom and Dad. They gazed at it fascinated, as if it were a work of wonder. It truly was an excellent painting.

"Can we get it framed?" Emmett asked.

"We'll get the best," Dad said softly.

Emmett took the painting to his room, sat on the edge of his bed and stared long and thoughtfully at the wall. He wasn't thinking where he'd hang the lovely painting. He was thinking about something else.

16

THE TEAMS in the Ice Cap League, Class D Division, finished the season as follows:

> Kodiaks
> Icebergs
> Polar Bears
> Penguins
> Eskimos
> Seals

The Kodiaks and the Polar Bears tangled Saturday A.M. at ten o'clock. The Kodiaks won. They would play the winner of the second game, Icebergs versus Penguins, which started at eleven o'clock. The winner of that game would be the champions of the Class D Division.

Emmett was in the starting lineup. While the captains of both teams discussed the court rules with the two referees, Emmett took a final look at the bench. Still no Mr. G. But he saw his Mom and Dad, and Charlene and Georgianne. He caught his Dad's smile, and flashed a quick one back.

The horn blew. The game was on. Rusty outjumped the Icebergs' willowy center, tapping the ball to Robin. Robin moved it upcourt and passed to Mickey, who shot a quick pass to Emmett. Emmett pivoted, leaped as if to throw an overhand shot, but fired to Rusty. Rusty drove in and laid the ball neatly against the backboard. Swish! A bucket!

Icebergs' ball out. They moved it to their backcourt. Emmett rushed in, intercepted a short pass, dribbled out of danger. He took it across the center line, then bounce-passed to Mickey. Mickey passed to Rusty near the baseline. Rusty took a set, flipping the ball with a graceful wrist motion. The ball hit the rim and bounded off. Rusty and Robin went in for the rebound. The Bergs got it. They moved it back into their territory. Seconds later the Bergs' No. 2 took a set and sank it.

"Come on, men!" cried Emmett. "Let's go!"

They began to drive, led by Emmett's spark. Rusty dumped in a long set, Emmett a layup. Mickey's fancy, close-to-the-floor dribbling had the Icebergs baffled. The quarter ended with the Penguins leading, 8 to 4.

"I'm going to remember what Mr. G. has told me," Emmett promised himself. "I can't be afraid. I'll just play hard, and play the best I can."

The Icebergs crept up slightly in the second quarter. In the third the Penguins rolled again. Ed Long put Johnny Clark in Mickey's place. Johnny fouled a man almost immediately. The Icebergs' player tossed in both free throws. A minute later Johnny made up for his foul, sinking a long shot that drew loud applause from the fans.

The fourth quarter was even scoring for both teams. The Penguins put the game into their pocket, 32 to 26.

"Now for the Kodiaks!" cried Robin Hood, as they ran to the shower room. "We can take them."

"They're tough," said Rusty. "Toughest in the league. The last time we played them we beat them by only one point. And they have improved."

"The tougher they are, the harder they

fall," quoted Robin Hood. "Besides, we have improved, too."

A heavy snowfall kept Emmett home all that next week, except for attending school. All that time he wondered about Mr. G. He hadn't seen Mr. G. since the little redhead had painted Emmett's picture.

The game with the Kodiaks rolled around quickly. Both teams looked strong and eager for the win as they came out on the court in their flashy uniforms, the Kodiaks in their red shirts and white trunks, the Penguins in their black satin suits.

The jump ball. The horn. The game was on. The Kodiaks took possession of the ball immediately. Seconds later they dumped in a basket. Penguins' ball. They moved it down-court. A layup missed for Rusty. The Kodiaks took the ball off the boards and rolled back upcourt — a pass, a short dribble, a pivot, then a shot. Swish! Another bucket.

Robin called time. He talked to his men. "Stop that Number 13," he said. "He's dead-eye!"

Time in. The Penguins moved cautiously now. Rusty passed to Robin, Robin to Emmett. A quick overhand to Rusty as the tall center ran for the basket. Rusty caught the ball and leaped. A layup!

That broke the spell. Both teams continued playing good ball, sinking baskets that drew applause after applause from the crowd. The score on the electric scoreboard teetered back and forth like a seesaw, first in the Kodiaks' favor, then in the Penguins'.

The quarters blinked off, one by one. Finally, a minute was left in the last quarter, with the Penguins leading, 39 to 38.

Kodiaks' ball. They passed upcourt. Emmett followed the ball closely. Then, like a quick, silent cat, he moved in and stole the ball!

He dribbled toward the center line. The Kodiaks came after him. He continued to dribble, matching Mickey, who was good at dribbling, too. He moved to the right, left, then right again — always keeping himself between the ball and an opponent.

"Get that ball! Get it before the clock runs out!" he heard a Kodiak man shout.

But they didn't get it. The horn blew, announcing the end of the game. The Penguins were the champs.

On his way home from the game with his family, Emmett stopped at Mr. G.'s apartment and knocked on the door. No answer.

A window slid open above his head.

"Is that you, Emmett?" said Mrs. Maxwell. "No use knocking. He hasn't been here in a week. Wish he'd stop in for a minute. Got a letter for him."

"A letter?" echoed Emmett.

"Yes. Just hold on a second." Mrs. Maxwell left. She soon returned with a letter and handed it to Emmett. "Don't think it's important. Looks like one of those advertisements. Take it. Maybe you'll see him before I do."

Emmett looked the letter over. It had a local postmark. In the upper lefthand corner was the name and address of the Fenway Museum of Art.

17

"I MUST find Mr. G.," said Emmett. "I must!"

But where could he look? Who knew where Mr. G. had gone? Perhaps he had gone back to New York. Emmett didn't want to believe that. Mr. G. wouldn't possibly go away permanently without saying good-by to his best friend, would he?

An idea flashed through Emmett's mind. The Sunset Spa. Mary Lee could tell him if Mr. G. had been in there recently.

Mary Lee recognized Emmett the moment he stood at the ice cream bar. "Hi! All alone today?"

Emmett smiled. "I am right now," he

said. "You remember Mr. G., don't you?"

"Mr. G.?" Her cheeks dimpled. "Yes, I do. Matter of fact, if you're looking for him, you might still catch him. He left here less than five minutes ago."

Emmett's brows shot up. "He did? Where did he go? Did he say?"

"He said he was on his way home. But first, he wanted to stop at the museum."

"The museum?" Emmett's heart started to pound. "Thank you!"

He ran out of the door and all the way up the street to the museum without stopping. He pulled open the large door and walked in, breathing hard. The place was crowded with people — men, women, and children.

Emmett began walking through the huge rooms, looking at everyone. The people were admiring the paintings on the

147

walls and the sculptures on tables placed throughout the building.

At last something bright and red attracted Emmett's eye. Emmett ran forward, brushing people's arms and almost knocking down a little girl in his haste.

" 'Scuse me!" he said.

Then he was standing beside Mr. G., who was looking at a painting of a covered bridge with a longing expression in his eyes. "Mr. G.!" said Emmett breathlessly. "I've been looking for you! Where have you been?"

"Emmett! My friend, you're all out of breath!" Mr. G. put out his hand, and Emmett grasped it. "I was on a trip up north. Was snowed in, couldn't get back till this morning. Sorry I didn't get to your basketball games, Emmett. How did you make out?"

Emmett smiled proudly. "We're champs of the D Division. We beat the Icebergs and then the Kodiaks."

"Well, for little birds you Penguins sure conquered some mighty monsters. Now tell me why you were so anxious to find me."

Emmett drew the letter out of his coat pocket. "This is for you, Mr. G.," he said. "Mrs. Maxwell gave it to me."

Mr. G. read the return address. "Hm-mm," he murmured. "What could this be?"

He opened one end of the envelope and pulled out the letter. He began to read silently. Then he cried out: "Emmett, what's this? Listen! 'Congratulations! Your painting, *Basketball Boy*, has won first prize in the regional art show. Enclosed is our check for five hundred dollars'!"

Emmett's eyes dimmed. A lump stuck in his throat. "Golly, Mr. G.!" he said.

"Emmett, you had that painting," said Mr. G., wide blue eyes staring. "It was you —"

Emmett nodded, and swallowed the lump in his throat. "Yes, Mr. G. I knew about the contest. Remember, I told you about it, but you wouldn't listen. I entered the painting for you. That is, Dad helped me. I thought it was very good. Mom and Dad thought it was, too. And look what happened. You won, Mr. G.! You won first prize!"

"Yes. Yes, I won. It's hard to believe, Emmett. I feel as if I'm dreaming all this." Mr. G.'s eyes became moist. He pulled the check out of the envelope. "Five hundred dollars! It's amazing, Emmett. I thought sure I was finished. I owe it to you, Emmett. You have restored my life. You have given me back the courage I needed. How can I ever thank you, Emmett?"

Emmett smiled. "You helped me, too, Mr. G. You saved my life once. And you gave me courage to play basketball. I guess we're even, Mr. G."

Mr. G. laughed. "Come. Let's see where that painting is."

They found it in the next room. But they couldn't get anywhere near it. Too many people were standing in front of the picture, looking at it, admiring it.

"I can barely see the ribbon pinned to it," said Mr. G. "But, jumping jackrabbits! I'm wasting time here! Let's go home! I must get started on another one!"

"Not me," said Emmett. "I'm going to get the Penguins to come see the painting!"